MAPPYS

IS UP TO MISCHIEF

Mila & Juna Albery

This is a work of fiction, names, characters and institutions are either products of the author's imagination or are used fictitiously. Any resemblance to actual persons, living or dead, is purely coincidental.

ISBN: 9781651802335

MAPPYS' FIRST WEEK

It's been a week now since Mappys tumbled out of my cell phone. Believe me, it was an incredibly turbulent week 'cause my cute little baby batsquirrgaroo has been up to mischief the whole time.

He doesn't do it on purpose, though. Mappys is just a baby, who wants to try as many things as possible. Playing the xylophone for example.

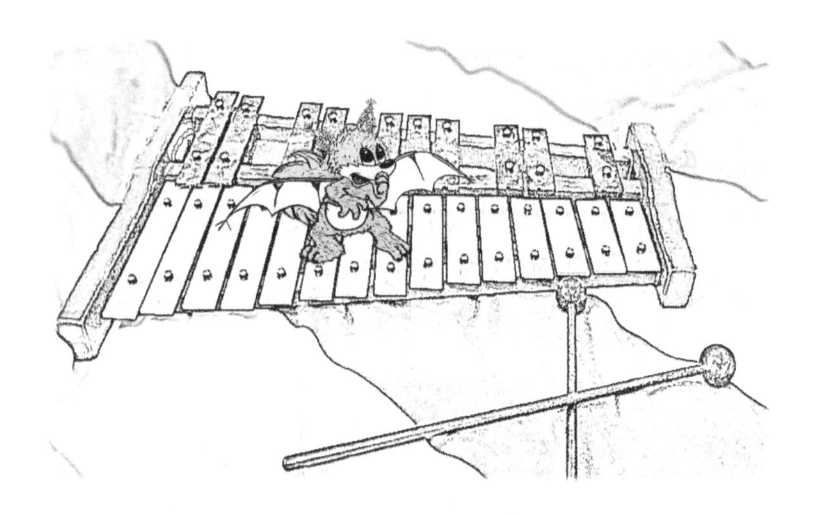

He does that simply by hopping. Now and then, one of his little paws gets stuck between the keys. Then he squeaks unhappily and I have to free him immediately.

He learns new things every day. Yesterday, he learned to use the toilet, the cat's toilet to be precise. It's a problem because we only have the one box for our cat Agatha. In any case, Agatha makes a huge fuss when she finds Mappys' contribution to her litter box.

Mom, who has no idea what's going on, is already quite irritated by our hysterical cat.

During the first week of his life, Mappys slept a lot. So it was easy to smuggle him to school in my schoolbag. I always made sure it was closed, and there were no problems—except this one time when we had to take a test in math. He squeaked and scratched inside my bag, and I had to drown his noises out the whole time. I shuffled my feet, creaked with my chair, coughed, growled and hummed.

My teacher, Mrs. Gieselbrecht, was so annoyed with me that she almost threw me out of the classroom. For that math test it wouldn't have made any difference. I couldn't concentrate on it anyway. I'm pretty sure I completely failed it.

But there is good news as well. My annoying little brother really kept the secret and hasn't told anyone about Mappys so far.

He loves to play with my baby, and helps me to hide him, or keep him away from Agatha.

Since breakfast I've been looking forward to when Emily will come over. She's my best friend, who lives in the neighborhood, and is the only one—besides my brother—who knows about Mappys' existence.

Finally the doorbell rings, and I run to the door. But it isn't Emily.

It's Alyssa.

Right, it's *Alyssa-weekend.* She is Andrew's daughter and since our stepdad moved in five years ago, she regularly comes every second weekend. She is fourteen already and a head taller than me.

"Oh . . . hi," I say.

She passes me without a word. Greetings are beneath her since the last few months.

"Dad?"

Andrew comes running.

"Hi sweetheart!"

"Will you drive me to the mall today? I'm invited to a party and have nothing to wear!"

"What party?" Andrew asks, and I can hear the disappointment in his voice.

"Dad, I told you, my friend Bianca . . ."

The doorbell rings again.

This time it's Emily.

She quickly greets my parents, and then we disappear into my room.

I close the door.

ALYSSA

Emily is awfully curious. She's hardly seen Mappys during the week. In school I didn't dare to let her look into my schoolbag, so the other kids wouldn't get curious as well. And in the afternoons, she wasn't allowed to come over this week because we had so much homework to do.

Unfortunately Emily isn't very good in school. But she's an awesome friend. Now she's fidgeting around beside me because she's so excited.

"Where is Mappys? You still hide him under the bed?"

I shake my head. "No, not anymore. That's too dangerous, in case Agatha might come in."

You simply can't trust our spoiled cat. She developed an unhealthy interest in my room lately. There are scratch marks on my door already. She's even been in my room twice, when someone didn't close the door properly. I found her on my desk, where she was greedily looking up at the box on top of my wardrobe.

That special box has been Mappys' home for a couple of days already. It's a sturdy plastic box, which I found in our basement. I arranged the box as conveniently as possible for Mappys.

He's still got my woolen hat as a bed and the little ball to play with. Besides that, I also gave him a little stuffed animal to cuddle with and a little bowl with water, in case he gets thirsty.

The box is high enough that Mappys can't climb out, but it's low enough to fit in between the wardrobe and the ceiling.

I'd love to give Mappys my old hamster cage, which is stored in the basement, but it wouldn't fit on top of the closet and Mom would immediately see it, which mustn't happen.

Still, I love the idea of having him safe in that cage, but he'd probably be terribly unhappy.

Carefully, I bring the box down.

My sweet little darling is awake and waves at me excitedly. I put the box on the bed, and Mappys squeaks impatiently.

He wants out.

Clear.

I reach out for him, and he crawls up my arm instantly.

"Cute," Emily whispers. "You think he would come to me too?"

"Try!" I say.

Emily stretches out her hand with her palm upwards.

Mappys makes a few hesitant steps at first, but then climbs Emily's arm up to her shoulder.

She is all smiles.

"What can he do already?"

"Well, climb up arms, use the litterbox, play the xylophone and play soccer." I proudly list his progress.

"Does he already eat different foods?" Emily wants to know.

"No, just corn. He refuses everything else." I answer a bit unhappily. I would have loved to find some other food, he likes.

"What did you try?"

"Everything. Just everything we've got at home. Yesterday, I even wanted to try Andrew's truffles."

"What are truffles?" Emily asks.

"They are like mushrooms, but very rare. And they smell strange. Anyway, they are awfully expensive, and Andrew caught me right when I opened the glass."

"Oh . . ." Emily's eyes widen.

"I stammered I always wanted to try them and just imagine, he was happy that I . . . wait, I wrote that down! Yeah, that *I was ready to make such exquisite culinary experiences at my young age already.*"

"Wow." Emily scratches her head. "And what does that mean?"

"No idea. I don't care. It sucked, though, that I actually had to try these truffles then!"

"And?" Emily asks curiously.

"Yucky." Just thinking about it, I have to make a face.

"Although they are so expensive?"

"Yes. Crazy, right? There are so many things that taste much better and are much cheaper. But adults are strange anyway. They like coffee as well . . ."

"And did Mappys try the tuffles?"

"Truffles," I correct her. "No, I'm still waiting for an opportunity."

"I can take care of him, and you go get them." Emily offers.

"Good idea," I say.

But the kitchen is crowded.

Mom unpacks groceries, while Toby

grabs at everything that's sweet, and Alyssa has a loud argument with Andrew.

"Come on, Daddy, all my friends are allowed to stay out until 10 p.m. I will be the only one who'll be picked up at 9."

"Ha ha, I'm sure, every parent gets to hear this . . ." Andrew can't be twisted around her finger that easily.

"No, Daddy, honestly, Melanie and Isa really are allowed . . ."

Oh yes, the party tonight. Alyssa's fighting for every minute. I'm secretly smiling 'cause I have an idea about how this is going to end.

"Maybe, but I'll certainly be picking you up at 9 p.m." Andrew can be quite stubborn, when push comes to shove. Alyssa starts crying, and I watch them interested. Will tears change Andrew's mind?

Doesn't look like it. He helps Mom put away the groceries, completely unimpressed.

"I'm going to the bathroom. And I don't want to be disturbed. Understood?" Alyssa suddenly yells at Toby.

"Yes . . ."

"You too?" This is directed to me.

I just nod. I know that already. She stays in the bathroom forever. And I mean for hours. First, she spreads out all her makeup stuff and then she needs hours to color her face. Afterward, she looks like a circus artist during carnival.

Today, she'll probably stay in there even longer, as the makeup won't stick to her wet face.

Anyway, the timing is bad for getting the truffles. So I give up my plan and return to Emily.

"I taught Mappys something!"

Emily beams. She's sitting with her legs up on my bed. Mappys is crouching in front of her and looks at her full of expectation.

"I call it the liana game."

"Show me!" I demand curiously.

"Okay, watch."

She lets some cord swing in front of his face.

"Snatch!" she tells him.

And Mappys actually snatches the cord, and she swings him to and fro until she lets him land on a pillow.

Mappys squeaks with joy.

"Awesome! Let me try."

I grab the cord.

We have a lot of fun, playing this game until Mappys gets tired. I put him into the woolen hat between us, and he falls asleep immediately.

Emily fishes her phone out of her pocket.

"Did your phone get fixed yet?" she asks.

"No, Andrew took it to the store, but they had to send it in and now we have to wait even longer." I roll my eyes.

"Crap," Emily says. "I wanted to play PettyPet-Favorites with you."

I nod, but I'm not even sure I want to play the game anymore. I was looking forward to this game so much, I only wanted to get a cell phone because of it. But since little Mappys tumbled out of this app, I'm not sure if I want it anymore. Mappys in the game could never be as cute as Mappys in real life, so . . .

"Come on, let's play with Nelly!" Emily says.

Nelly is a bearowlpard. A mixture of bear, owl and leopard. A very well done mixture! She's an exceptionally clever pet!

"Nelly is on level 4 already," Emily explains proudly. "She's eating five different foods and understands all basic tasks. Look."

Nelly appears on the display and dances.

"Sit," Emily commands, and Nelly sits down immediately.

"Give paw," Emily says, and Nelly stretches out her paw.

Lie down, *jump* and *turn around* all work out flawlessly.

"She even can *fall asleep*," Emily brags. Nelly instantly curls herself up into a ball and starts snoring.

I'm really impressed.

"And she already won two tournaments." Emily points to the two trophies in the background.

"Cool."

"Should we play a partner tournament? I didn't dare do that so far." Emily suggests.

"What's that?"

"Nelly has to successfully complete certain tasks with my help."

"Ok, let's try." I agree.

Emily smiles and clicks on *accept partner tournament*.

"Oh, my gosh! We have to compete against an elefoxtiger. That's gonna be tough."

I watch spellbound. Brix, the elefoxtiger, is twice the size of Nelly. They are both equally good at the basic training. Now comes the main task. The pets must find their reward in the arena. The owner must lead them on with *left, right, ahead, back, quick* and *slow*. The pet, which snatches its reward with its snout first, may keep it and wins.

Emily is extremely nervous.

She mixes up left and right and gives her commands way too hectically. Nelly stumbles and falls. She hurts one of her front paws and Emily has to activate the first aid kit, which takes precious time. Besides, Nelly is limping now and looks terribly unhappy. Emily is close to tears.

Suddenly a message pops up, saying that Brix, the elefoxtiger, sprained her ankle and has to pause for one day.

Emily's eyes widen.

"Poor thing!"

Now, Nelly can finish her task without being rushed, after she's been treated for her injury. Emily's commands are clearly and effectively now, and Nelly calmly limps towards the treasure box. The box contains a trophy, which Nelly holds up proudly and a chocolate mouse, which she eats happily.

Another message pops up on the display.

Emily squeaks with joy, but a sudden scream from the bathroom drowns out everything else.

MAKEUP MAYHEM

The scream is so piercing that it makes my hair stand on end.

"Daaaaddy . . .!"

Alyssa without a doubt.

My eyes search the woolen hat right away and—it is empty.

I swallow and feel the panic rise.

The door is left ajar. How could that happen? I was so spellbound by Nelly's tournament that I didn't realize when Mappys escaped.

Where is he?

And where is Agatha?

I run through the hallway where a crying Alyssa passes me and further to the bathroom. There, the first thing I do is catch Agatha. She hisses and scratches like mad, but I keep on holding her firmly. Her snout is empty which is a good sign.

Then my gaze falls on the sink. Oh my God, what happened here?

Eye shadow, pencils, lipsticks and powder boxes lie around, the colors crumbled and smeared all over the place.

If you look closely, you can see tiny paw prints between the color stains. I push Agatha out of the bathroom and quickly try to remove the paw tracks with my fingers. But they end up smeared all over the place.

"Mappys," I whisper.

Squeak.

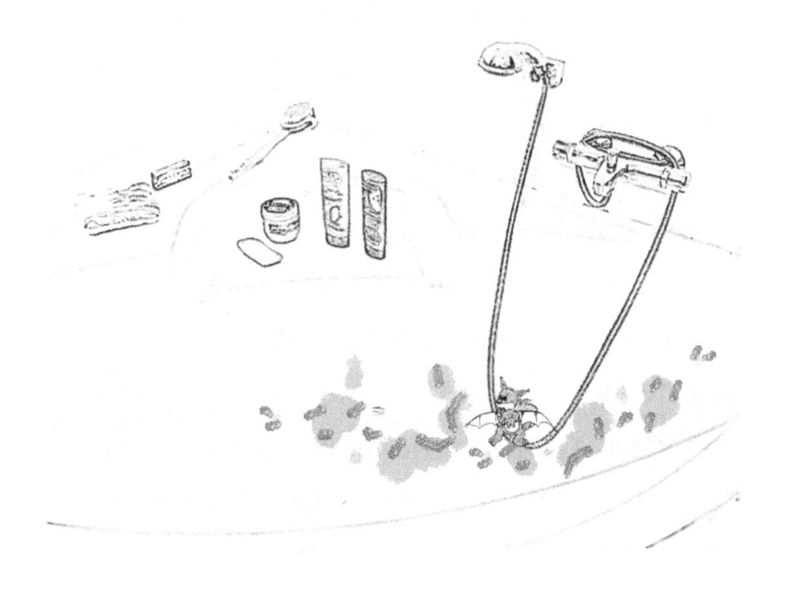

Now, I see him. He landed in the tub which is fortunately empty, but from which he can't get out anymore. I grab him and hide him in my hood before Alyssa comes back with Andrew and Mom.

"I just went to the toilet shortly, now look what she did," Alyssa complains.

"Me? Why me?"

"Who else?"

"But . . . "I don't know what to say.

"Daddy, look, she's still got the color on her hands." Alyssa points at me.

They all stare at my color tainted fingers now.

"I . . . well . . . ," I stammer.

"Clean yourself up and the sink as well," Mom says. "We'll talk later."

Alyssa grabs whatever is not broken from her makeup stuff and puts it into her beauty case. While she throws an angry look at me, she disposes of the rest.

Only now can I even use the sink. The eye shadow is sticking on my skin and it

takes me a while to get my hands clean.
At least Mappys is quiet in my hood.

PUNISHMENT

All three are sitting around the table—Mom, Andrew and Alyssa. Alyssa has an especially acrimonious expression on her face.

"Charlie," Mom starts, "what do you have to say for yourself?"

Yeah, what? What should I say?

"I don't know . . . "

"Why did you ruin Alyssa's makeup?"

I lower my gaze. Somehow, it actually is my fault. I left the door open, and I was distracted.

I didn't pay enough attention to Mappys. He could have been hurt. He could have even been eaten by Agatha.

Oh my God, I'd never forgive myself for that.

Just thinking about it, I start to cry.

"You don't have to cry," Andrew says and pets my hair. "Everyone makes a mistake now and then, right Alyssa?"

Alyssa throws me an evil look.

I pout and catch some of my tears with my lips.

They taste salty.

"Charlie certainly won't do that again, right?" Andrew says and looks at me, then at Alyssa.

I nod.

"I'm sorry", I say and I mean it. Even if my family doesn't really know what I'm sorry for.

Suddenly, Toby bursts in.

"Alyssa should apologize as well. She always insults me when no one can hear it!" he demands.

"Is that true?" Andrew asks and Alyssa denies it, of course.

But Mom looks concerned.

Andrew gets up with a sigh.

"Come on, we're going to the mall. There you can get some new makeup stuff."

Alyssa beams instantly and Toby wants to use the situation in his favor as well.

"Can I watch TV?"

Mom nods.

To me she doesn't say another word.

I'm sure I will get my punishment. I'll probably be grounded. But the feeling that I disappointed her is even worse.

It makes me sad. I go back to my room and say good bye to Emily, who has to go back home now. Then I put Mappys back in his box, which I put up on the wardrobe again. This time, I thoroughly close the door and go to clean the bathroom.

IN THE STUDIO

I lie in bed and stare at the ceiling.

I cleaned the bathroom for more than an hour. Mappys really did a great job with smearing the stuff all over the place.

Emily says that PettyPet-pets are only that exhausting as long as they are babies. If you keep them busy, they learn quickly and the more they can do, the less mischief they make. Unless they get bored. Or they just do it for fun. Some are like that.

It's quiet in our house now. Andrew and Alyssa are still gone, Toby is watching TV and Mom . . .

Hmm, where is Mom?

Probably in her studio. It's a very bright room that Andrew built just for her. She's painting there and she loves doing that.

I hear a gentle squeak from the box on my wardrobe.

So, Mappys is awake again.

He doesn't sleep as much during the day anymore, which means he's sleeping through the nights. That is definitely a relief.

I get the box from the closet and an excited little pet waves at me and quickly climbs into my hood. I guess I'll let him surf on the robotic vacuum cleaner. He loves that and maybe Mom will forgive me if I clean up my room.

I pick up all the stuff off the floor and go get Bob, our vacuuming robot. Mappys squeaks with joy when I put him down. He runs towards Bob immediately. The robot is round and low enough for Mappys to climb up without any help.

He sits down in the middle and looks at me hopefully.

I press the START button. Bob starts driving around and the two little lights on his front blink wildly.

Mappys squeals with excitement and the two of them are busy for the next half hour.

I decide to look for Mom. I firmly close the door from the outside and even stick a note on it.

KEEP OUT!
BOB'S WORKING

As expected, I find Mom in the studio. She doesn't even notice when I slip in. Andrew always says the world could fall apart while Mom is painting, and she wouldn't even notice.

I snuggle up to her from behind, and she jumps.

Then she laughs.

"You wanna paint as well, Charlie?"

"Yes, I'd love to."

I got my own little easel last Christmas, but I hardly ever use it.

Mom gives me a canvas, and I start selecting the colors.

Though I don't have any idea what to paint, my hands pick color after color and soon the palette is full. Then I search for a soft paintbrush and get started.

"That's really nice," Mom says all of a sudden, and I get startled. Now, I'm just like her. I forgot space and time while painting.

Mom stands behind me and admires my work.

"How cute . . . what kind of animal is that, Charlie? A squirrel with wings? And it's got a little pouch as well!"

Oh no, without even thinking I painted a picture of Mappys, and Mom eyes him very interested.

"Oops," I say, "my imagination obviously ran awry."

"That's what painting is for." Mom smiles at me.

My gaze falls on the clock. Oh no, I've been painting for more than two hours. I urgently have to look after Mappys. I just hope he didn't get into mischief again.

I leave Mom at the studio and run by Toby, who has fallen asleep in front of the TV.

There is no sound coming from my room.

Hopefully, that's a good sign!

PAPER!

I carefully open my door and look inside.

Oh my gosh!

What a mess!

The whole room is full with white paper snippets.

Mappys obviously found my paper supply and wanted to show me how good he is at tearing paper apart.

And so much!

Fortunately, my school bag is closed, otherwise he probably would have gotten my notebooks as well.

Bob, who could have cleaned up the mess—at least what's on the ground—lies in the middle of the room, apathetically. His eyes aren't sparkling anymore. His battery is empty.

Crap!

Mappys crawls up on me, beaming. Seems like he wants to be complimented for his work.

"Tearing paper is not good, Mappys," I tell him.

He still tries for a while to get some approval, and eventually I pet him, as I can't be mad at him anyway. He's content and climbs back into my hood.

I go get a garbage bag. Mappys now enthusiastically helps to put every snippet into the bag.

I applaud him for every snippet he throws in and he really loves this game.

Again, I think longingly about the hamster cage in the basement. It would make my life so much easier.

Suddenly, I hear Agatha meowing and scratching at the door. Mappys looks up, drops all the snippets and scurries into my hood again.

"Agatha!" Mom yells. "Will you stop that!"

She opens the door. Agatha rushes in and jumps up on me. I back off and stumble over the lifeless Bob. While trying not to fall, I end up tearing down the floor lamp in the corner. We both fall to the ground and I instantly close my eyes, as not to be hit by shards of glass.

Mom covers her face in her hands.

"Oh my God, Charlie!"

Then she furiously turns to the cat.

"Agatha, what's wrong with you?"

She grabs the angry cat and throws her right out of the window.

"I don't know what to do anymore with this crazy cat! Did you hurt yourself?"

Mom looks at me worried.

It doesn't hurt anywhere. I reach into my hood to see if Mappys is fine as well, but it's empty.

"I'm fine," I murmur, though nothing is fine. Mappys obviously fled. At least Agatha is in the garden now, so he's safe from her anyway.

TOBY

I'm snacking on yogurt with fruit which Mom has lovingly cut for me. And Toby, who never skips an opportunity to spill yogurt all over himself, is sitting next to me.

Mappys is still gone. Maybe he's sleeping in his hiding place. As long as Agatha is outside, it's all good.

Andrew comes home. Alone. He already took Alyssa to the birthday party. There was a makeup workshop in the mall, which turned out to be exactly what she needed.

After dinner, Andrew leaves again to pick Alyssa up and I start looking out for Mappys. I need to find him quickly because sooner or later Mom will let Agatha in again.

I don't need to search for long, though. Toby comes to me, his face pale, his eyes wet.

"Charlie," he gasps. "Charlie, come with me."

His room is a total mess.

Everything, really everything is covered with scraps of paper.

When Mappys sees me, he happily runs toward me. Even though he created such chaos, I'm happy to have him back. He crawls into my hood, and I go get another garbage bag.

Toby and I sweep the snippets off the floor while Mappys collects single pieces. He wants to be rewarded for every snippet. It's obvious that he loves this game.

How can I break him of this habit?

Suddenly, Toby starts howling like a

wolf. His schoolbag was open and Mappys got a hold of his finished homework.

Now he has to do everything again.

Of course, I promised to help him. It's gonna be a long night.

When Mom takes me to bed this evening, we cuddle like always. Usually I talk about the teachers or the other kids, and she listens to everything I've got on my mind.

But today, she first made it clear that I'm grounded for a week. I understand that. Then she nags on about Agatha and I listen. Seems like this evening we switched roles.

Actually our cat didn't do anything wrong, though. A cat is a cat. Mice, birds and squirrels will be hunted. That's why she practices her whole life climbing trees.

"What shall I do? I can't leave her outside all night," Mom whines.

"I'm sure it's just a phase." I comfort her.

We definitely did switch parts.

Mom sighs and wishes me a good night. "Strange things are happening around here lately," she says, already halfway out of the door.

So true.

At least I know the reason for it. It's the tiny, fluffy, and blissfully sleeping animal in my hat on top of the wardrobe.

As soon as Mom left the room, I get Mappys down and put him on my bed.

I wait for a short while, then sneak over to Toby's room to help him do his homework again.

SUNDAY

At breakfast I can hardly keep my eyes open. Toby is the same. We both were up until long after midnight and finished his homework.

"What's wrong with the two of you?" Mom's wondering.

"Must be the fall tiredness," I say.

Alyssa yawns as well.

"There's something to that," she says and I look up in surprise. She's never agreed to anything I've said so far.

"We actually wanted to go hiking with the three of you today . . . " Andrew starts and a collective moaning fills the room.

"Without me," Alyssa growls.

"Without me," I echo.

"Without . . ." Toby starts, but Mom interrupts.

"Got it. What else do you want to do then?"

"Sleep!"

"Watch TV!"

"Nothing . . ."

We all answer at the same time—a disharmonic canon.

"Maybe bake a cake in the afternoon?" I suggest, smiling at Mom, and she nods.

"Alright, we'll do that."

All of a sudden, Agatha jumps on the table right in between the butter and the jam. She hisses.

We all jump and Mom furiously gets up from her chair.

"You crazy cat, just when I let you in . . ."

She grabs Agatha and dashes toward the terrace door. Andrew opens it and Agatha is on her way again.

I start to feel sorry for her.

If she doesn't calm down soon, she'll be in for a cold winter.

After breakfast, I snuggle up to Mappys in my bed and fall asleep quickly. When I open my eyes again, Emily is sitting beside me.

"Your mom let me in," she says by way of greeting. "I'm only allowed to stay for a short *hello*, though, since you are grounded. Look, I found some of the old stuff for my dolls."

She empties a basket on my bed. I yawn and stretch while she picks out some tiny blue overalls.

"Look at those, how cute."

We find a lot of stuff in Mappys' size, although we'll have to cut a hole into some of them for his fluffy tail.

Mappys loves to be the center of the attention. Then, I remember the most important question: "How can I stop Mappys from tearing paper apart?"

"Hm . . . PettyPet has a couple of options if the pet doesn't behave. You can punish your pet by not feeding it or not playing with it. In any case, you can't reward it. When Nelly misbehaves, I loudly say *wrong* and then ignore her for three hours."

"Pheeew . . . to ignore Mappys for three hours is more a punishment for me!" I complain.

"Yes," Emily says precociously. "When parents have to punish their kids, it's a punishment for them as well."

"Where'd you get that from?"

"From my mom," Emily says and leaves.

That's interesting. Now I´m pondering—does Mom suffer as well when I am grounded?

SCHOOL

As time passes I become a very well organized batsquirrgaroo-mom. Right after getting up I fed Mappys, put him on the cat toilet and hide him in his hat-bed in my school bag.

Unfortunately, things are not going all too well in school right now. First thing in the morning our teacher, Mrs. Giesel-brecht, returns the math test. The one I screwed up so badly on. As feared, I got the worst possible grade. I firmly bite my lips to hold back tears, but they still run down my face. Unhappily, I stuff the test into my school bag.

The bell rings. Break!

Emily comes over to comfort me,

though her own test isn't that much better.

The next two hours is gym. I like that, especially when we play ball games. I'm good at them and they put me in a good mood. But today of all days we're doing gymnastics.

That means endless stretching and bending. We all moan when Mrs. Gieselbrecht announces that we're supposed to run in circles as well. Running for no reason is not fun at all. There isn't any sense of achievement like there is in ball games.

After the fourth round, I'm starting to sweat. Not because I'm exhausted, but because I'm suddenly not sure if I closed my school bag properly when I put my math test inside.

What if Mappys climbs around in the classroom?

I need to go check immediately.

I run for the exit and silently slip into the locker room, where I put on my sweater and pants. Although I can hardly breathe anymore, I run through the building to our class room.

The door is closed.

Carefully, I open it and look inside.

Oh no, no, no!

Mappys is sitting on the teacher's desk and has ripped the class-register into pieces. A hundred tiny pieces! Of all things, this book is where our teacher writes down our grades, if someone is absent and all kinds of other important stuff.

I can't believe it. What a mess! There'll be trouble! A lot of it!

Mappys beams at me. He is obviously proud of his doing.

What am I supposed to do?

While I'm still standing there helplessly and ruffle my hair, the door opens. I quickly turn around to hide Mappys with my body. It's Mrs Gieselbrecht.

"Charlie! There you are! Why did you run away?"

I back up until I can feel the teacher's desk behind me, and then I reach behind my back.

"Well, I . . . I . . .," I stammer and feel as Mappys climbs into my palm.

"Holy John!" My teacher suddenly yells. "What happened here?"

I move toward my desk.

Mrs. Gieselbrecht is about to comprehend the extent and the significance of the damage.

"Charlie, oh my God, have you completely . . ."

While she's at a loss for words, I back up further until I stand in front of my school bag. I crouch and let Mappys slip inside.

Then I sit down on the floor, close the bag and start crying.

"Charlie, why did you tear the class-register apart?" Mrs. Gieselbrecht comes towards me, filled with indignation. "Just because of the bad grade? You're making it even worse. I'll have to report the torn book to the principal."

Well, this is possibly the worst day of my life. My teacher takes me, the book, and the snippets to the principal, who gives me the same speech again. Then, she calls my mom and asks her to come.

I have to sit on a chair and wait.

Mom is already pale when she comes into the room.

"Charlie, what . . ."

The principal interrupts and explains in detail what happened. Well, what she thinks happened, not what really happened.

I've never seen Mom so shaken to the core, and that makes me cry again.

How I would love to tell her the truth! Then she wouldn't have to believe her daughter's gone mad. But what would happen to Mappys then?

So I just sniff and promise to never do something like that again.

I don't get any further punishment.

I think Mom doesn't really know what to do with this daughter, who's up to so much mischief all of a sudden.

I'm grounded anyway, which is not that bad since I love spending time in my room with Mappys.

The only inconvenience is that Emily is not allowed to see me. Luckily, she already told me how to stop Mappys from shredding paper.

I will practice with him every afternoon now.

ORANGES!

Today is already Friday, and I'm really proud. Mappys hasn't torn up any paper for the past two days.

It's time to reward him.

I'll give the expensive truffles one more try. This time I manage to take a piece out of the glass without being seen and bring it to my room. I also grab an orange I found in the fruit basket.

He refuses the truffles and I'm relieved. I'm even more happy when he takes a bite from the orange. He eats a whole slice except for the peel.

Great! Now I can feed him corn and oranges.

And he's learned something new as well: Jump!

It looks really cute when he tries to jump onto something. He then eagerly flaps his wings to gain momentum. He can't fly yet, but it looks like this jumping is his first attempt. He can already make it from my chair to my desk.

Sometimes he knocks things over while he jumps, but I know he doesn't do it on purpose.

Tomorrow is *Daddy-weekend* again. Mappys will come with me for the second time already. It's unbelievable how quickly the first two weeks have flown by.

BATHING DAY

After just ten minutes in the car, Toby spilled the news about my problems at school. I throw him an angry glance. I'd rather kick him in his leg. I'm really surprised he hasn't given away the secret about Mappys yet. Now, I have to defend myself because of the torn class-register again and, of course, Daddy doesn't understand it either.

Aunt Renee is already waiting for us in Daddy's apartment and fortunately no one brings up the school topic again.

My aunt shows me her new jacket with a fluffy warm hood and asks if I'd like to have one as well.

Hmm . . . Mappys would love this soft hood a lot, so "Yes, gladly."

Toby wants to try out a new computer game, which I'm not interested in, so I decide to take a long bath.

Mappys loves to splash in the water and luckily the bathroom door can be locked.

I let the water in and take one of Toby's little boats. Then, I put Mappys inside.

He loves that. He could ride on the foam waves for hours. Recently, he realized that he loves gliding down from the rim of the tub. With an enthusiastic squeak he disappears into the foam. I don't even know if he can swim 'cause I always catch him immediately.

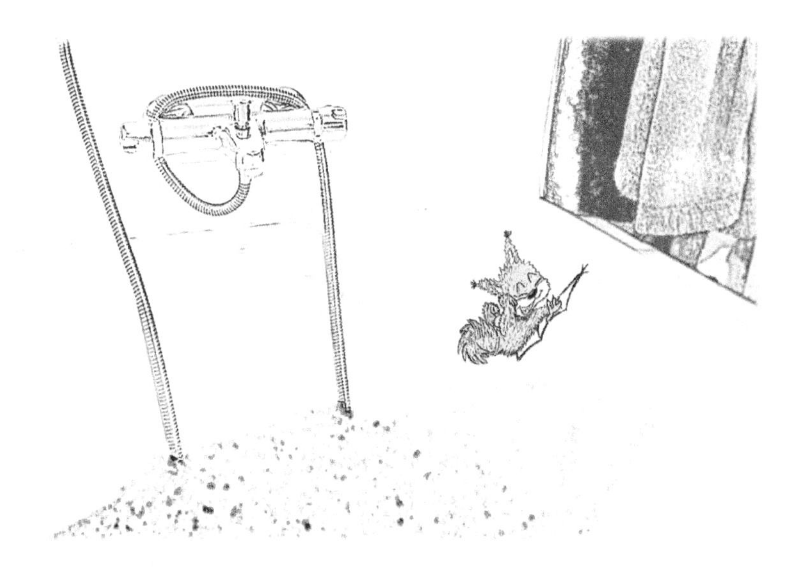

What he can't take at all is the drying afterward. Neither with the towel, nor with the hairdryer. It's necessary, though, so he doesn't get a cold. A cold is certainly no fun for such a small batsquirrgaroo.

Now, he's yawning.

Yes, playing and bathing is tiring. I put him into the warm woolen hat and hide him between two pillows in my bed.

Meanwhile, in the living room they're preparing a board game. It's one of my favorite ones where you're supposed to build towns, streets and ships.

All four of us are playing, and soon it's clear that Aunt Renee is going to lose. She doesn't like that at all. Soon she gives up and says good bye.

Toby begs us to continue playing, and I agree, as I'm about to win. I do actually beat Daddy and Toby.

We kids clear the table afterward, and Daddy starts cooking.

I grab a book and lay down on my bed.

The woolen hat between my pillows lies there quietly. I look at it and freeze.

The hat is empty.

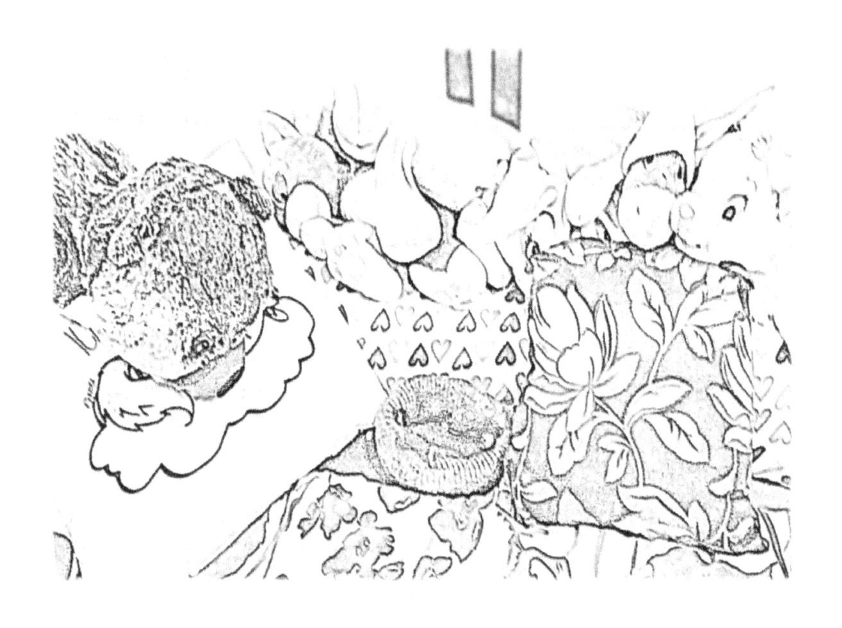

Oh, no! Not again! Where is he now?

Keep cool, I say to myself, there is no Agatha here.

No way, I can concentrate on reading anymore. Instead, I start searching the room for Mappys.

I whisper his name, look in every corner and in every crevasse.

Nothing.

Nothing.

Nothing.

Still nothing.

Crap!

Did he go to the bathroom again 'cause he loves splashing so much?

I check the bathroom. *Meticulously.* That's another word Andrew taught me. Sounds very complicated, but it just means very accurate. No matter how *meticulously* I search the bathroom though, there is no trace of Mappys.

I close the door behind me and look around. Daddy's bedroom door is open, so I have to search there as well. First of all I crawl under the bed.

"Mappys?"

Nothing.

Oh my gosh, is it dusty here! Extremely! I have to sneeze and hit my head on the bed frame. Suddenly, Toby stands in the door and picks his nose.

"What are you doing here?" he asks without interrupting his exciting activity.

I get up from under the bed.

"Mappys is gone!"

"Oh." Toby's eyes widen and he stops picking his nose. "I can help you search for him."

We check behind the curtains, but he isn't there either. There aren't any more hiding places in Daddy's bedroom, so we close this door and continue our search in the living room.

Dad is cooking in the kitchen. The meat is sizzling quite loudly and hopefully needs his full attention. After all he shouldn't notice that we are searching his whole apartment.

All the searching doesn't help, though. We cannot find Mappys in the living room, nor in the hallway, nor in the bathroom.

Meanwhile, I'm really desperate.

Mappys doesn't show up the rest of the evening, and I'm terribly worried.

AUNT RENEE

Daddy is a little hurt because I have no appetite, and he really went out of his way with the cooking.

My thoughts are with Mappys, though. Where is he?

I can't stop thinking about him. When Daddy disappears into the kitchen again to wash the dishes, I start searching for Mappys again.

I check every pillow and look behind every book on the shelf for the second time.

Nothing.

Toby is moody as well, and Daddy asks us in vain what's wrong with us.

At 9 p.m. he sends us to bed. While saying good night, his cell rings all of a sudden.

"Hi Renee . . . what? Nonsense!"

Dad rolls his eyes.

I look at him curiously.

"Renee, please calm down . . . certainly not . . . yes, I'll check that out tomorrow."

What's going on?

"What's the matter with Aunt Renee?" I ask Daddy after he ended the call.

Dad rolls his eyes again.

"Sometimes, she's a little hyped up, you know her. A couple of things fell from the shelf in her room, and now she thinks something paranormal is happening."

"Paranormal?" I ask.

"Yes, like ghosts and stuff," Daddy explains.

"Oh . . . oho!" I have a sneaking suspicion. "What exactly happened?"

"A framed photograph of Grandpa and a little porcelain angel fell off the shelf. I think they were on the edge, and when she bumped into it . . ."

"Yes, that can happen!"

Oh, I'm so happy 'cause now I know where Mappys is!

Of course! The fluffy hood on her jacket probably lured him in. He climbed in and fell asleep. It must have been like that.

"Let me call her!" I beg. "I know how I can help her."

"Yeah?" Dad looks at me, puzzled.

"Yes. Emily's mom is the same. She's always imagining things as well and she has joss sticks that help."

"Really?" Dad eyes me skeptically.

"Yes, seriously, well if you believe in it."

"Okay." Daddy gives in and dials Aunt Renee's number. When she picks up, he gives me the phone.

"Hi Aunt Renee, things have been falling off your shelf?"

"Yes, just imagine, all by themselves!" She sounds very excited. "And all the blossoms of a plant fell off. That's not normal!"

Blossoms?

Does Mappys pluck off blossoms now? I wouldn't put it past him.

"The same happened to Emily's mom once. She bought special joss sticks, and it never happened again," I lie confidently.

"That's great! Where do I get these joss sticks from?"

She bought it. Yes!

"I can bring them to you tomorrow morning," I say quickly.

"Oh, that's very nice of you. Thank you," Aunt Renee says gratefully.

Daddy compliments me as well 'cause I'm so helpful. Although I can see, what he thinks about the whole matter.

"You have to help one another in the family," I say.

He nods and promises to bring me to Emily, first thing tomorrow morning.

Until then, I need a plan.

An awesome plan.

A plan that has to work out.

Somehow, we have to lure Aunt Renee out of her apartment, so we can find Mappys!

THE PLAN

I hardly slept because I was so worried. First of all, since I didn't know whether Mappys was okay at Aunt Renee's. Secondly 'cause I kept thinking about how to lure Aunt Renee out of her own apartment.

Best would be to convince Dad to go for a walk with Aunt Renee while we fumigate her apartment.

But before that I have to call Emily. I retreat into my room and close the door, 'cause Daddy shouldn't hear what I'm going to tell her.

Emily starts to giggle immediately. She finds it unbelievably funny that her mom's joss sticks will be good for something after all. She promises me to beg her mom for some, and we agree that I'll come pick her up in half an hour.

Toby's excited as well. It's obvious. He can't sit still even for a moment, and he won't stop talking.

Daddy is stunned by our eagerness to help his sister. His clumsy sister, as he points out. It's clear that he still doesn't know what to make of it. He probably thinks that Emily's joss sticks won't do much against Aunt Renee's imaginary ghosts.

"Well, it won't hurt either," he murmurs as we climb into the car.

Emily is already waiting for us with a big bag. Her Mom stands proudly beside her.

"I packed candles and gold dust as well," she explains and Emily is all smiles.

We thank her and take Emily with us. She's playing her part really well. In less than two minutes, she convinces Daddy to lure Aunt Renee out of her apartment.

"You know, it only works if there is nobody in the room who's afraid of ghosts," Emily says very convincing.

Dad just nods. Whatever he is thinking he keeps to himself. He probably doesn't want to ruin our fun. "You won't light anything, right?"

"Just the joss sticks," Emily answers. "We don't need the candles. We'll just walk through the apartment with the joss sticks and the gold dust."

Daddy nods again, and soon we are at Aunt Renee's.

Aunt Renee opens the door with dark circles under her eyes.

"It's so nice of you that you came! The night was terrible," she complains while hanging up our jackets.

"Did any more things fall to the ground?" I ask.

"No, but I still couldn't sleep." Aunt Renee unhappily scratches her head.

"There were strange noises in my bedroom," she whispers.

"Yes? What kind of noises?" I already have a certain suspicion.

"Scratching and squeaking like from a mouse."

My heart skips a beat. Now, I'm definitely sure that Mappys is hiding somewhere in her apartment.

"And did you check?" Daddy asks.

"Yes, sure I checked with a flashlight under the bed. But I didn't see anything. Hey, I'm not crazy—I live on the third floor, there can't be any mice."

Yeah, probably not.

Emily unpacks her bag at the table and Aunt Renee curiously eyes everything. The joss sticks as well as the strangely scented candles.

Daddy looks doubtfully around the room. First at the smelly things on the table, then at his sister.

"I do have garlic if that helps," Auntie says all of a sudden.

Emily's mouth twitches. She's obviously having a hard time not to giggle.

"There are no traces of vampires, right?" she asks.

"Traces?" Aunt Renee's eyes widen.

"Yes, like bites for example."

"Hmm . . . no." She's blushing a little.

"Come on, lets take a walk around the block," Daddy suggests.

"Certainly not. I want to watch what they are doing." Aunt Renee is outraged.

"Okay." Daddy sits down.

We secretly beckon to him that they should leave.

"You know," he finally says. "I thought we might stop by the bakery . . ."

"You think so?" Aunt Renee seems to be more interested now.

"Yes, they make a delicious Tiramisu."

"That's right . . ." Now Aunt Renee looks excited.

"Will you bring some for us as well, please?" I say quickly.

"Please, please, please!"

"We'll only start when you're back again," Emily promises and looks at her with big puppy eyes.

Daddy frowns and I notice that he realizes the contradiction. In the car Emily said Aunt Renee mustn't be in the room for the ceremony to work.

"But . . ." he starts when I interrupt him quickly.

"Please Daddy, I'd love to have a strawberry yogurt cake."

"And a chocolate cake for me," Toby shouts.

"Okay, okay, we'll bring you some," says Aunt Renee, who has got the biggest sweet tooth of us all.

"What do you want?" she asks Emily.

"Applestrudel."

"Okay." Dad and Aunt Renee leave.

Dad throws me a warning glance. That's probably supposed to mean: Don't light the apartment on fire!

SAVING MAPPYS

Pheeew . . . finally!

Dad and Aunt Renee left. I lean against the entrance door, relieved.

"Come on, let's find Mappys!"

I start in the bedroom. But all I find under the bed is a lot of dust. It makes me sneeze immediately.

I check the living room, while Emily and Toby search in the kitchen. I look under every pillow, on every shelf and under the couch.

Nothing.

I rummage through the shelf beside the mirror in the hallway.

Nothing.

Maybe Mappys is behind the curtains? But I search in vain there as well. Emily and Toby don't find anything in the kitchen either. Last room I check is the bathroom.

Again nothing.

"Maybe he is hiding somewhere and fell asleep," I say quite desperate.

"Then we'll have to wake him up," Emily suggests.

"Yes, we can call him." Toby starts right away.

"Mappys!"

Now we check every room again, while shouting loudly.

Ten minutes later we stop.

"He can't hear us," I say sadly.

"Or he isn't here," Toby assumes.

"But where is he?" Emily turns in circles with a questioning expression on her face.

"He must be here." I say desperately. "Maybe he's in a wardrobe?"

"How would he have gotten in there?" Emily asks.

"Maybe Aunt Renee left a wardrobe door open and he slipped in? And now he can't get out again."

That was actually my last hope.

"Ok, let's search all wardrobes and cabinets."

"I'll check the kitchen!" Toby, who has already found some chocolate bars, grins.

"Well, I'll check the living room," says Emily.

So I'm left with the bedroom.

The biggest wardrobe is in there. When I open it, shoes cover the floor. I look in every single one of them.

Nothing.

Maybe Mappys is stuck between the socks and underwear?

Again nothing.

Now there is only the part left where the clothes are hung up. There are lots of dresses and jackets. I check every pocket and every hood, but they are all empty.

In the back corner I see a basket. With warm gloves and woolen hats.

Woolen hats!

I take them out carefully and . . .

. . . finally!

In the third hat I find my little darling.

Sleeping.

"Mappys," I whisper happily and pet his fur.

He opens his eyes, yawns and beams at me. He climbs up to my face immediately and snuggles up to my cheek.

I don't have words to describe how happy I am. Tears well up in my eyes, and I quickly wipe them away with my sleeve. Mappys coos and rubs his little snout against my cheek.

That's so cute.

Just in time, I remember that we need to hurry, and I put him into my hood.

I enter the living room again just when Daddy and Aunt Renee come through the door.

Emily and Toby look at me desperately.

I quickly show them thumbs up and point at my hood.

"You're just in time," I say to Daddy and Aunt Renee. "We can start fumigating now, and then we'll eat the cake."

Emily beams and does her very best.

She lights the joss sticks and makes all kinds of moves that almost look like dancing while singing strange melodies. After five minutes, she sits down at the kitchen table.

"Finished! All ghosts are gone!"

"Really? That quick?" Aunt Renee asks stunned.

"Yes," Emily assures her. "All it takes are joss sticks, gold dust and the right magic spell."

"You'll sleep like a baby again," I add.

Toby already started to eat his chocolate cake.

"Tastes great!"

I can say the same about my strawberry yogurt cake, and Emily happily makes a grab at her applestrudel. She smiles with her full mouth, tells ghost stories from her mother and assures us once again, that joss sticks and gold dust would help against anything. That's why she blows some of it into Aunt Renee's hair when we say good bye. I have to turn away so nobody notices my giggling.

We take Emily home, and afterward, we have a cozy evening at Dad's.

Toby comes to my room. I think he's as happy as I am that Mappys is back.

Even though it's sometimes really exhausting, I can't imagine my life without my little batsquirrgaroo.

Although his childhood days aren't over yet and he'll probably be responsible for a lot more awkward situations, I'm more than happy to have him.

DEAR READERS!

If you want to know how it all began, please read

Volume 1 Mappys Tumbles Into Life.

If you want to hear more about the adventures of Charlie and Mappys, please follow Mila Albery on Amazon.

Mappys would really appreciate your review on Amazon!

For personal messages please don't hesitate to write to: mila.albery@gmx.at

AUTHOR'S NOTE

Mila Albery worked together with her daughter Juna to create this story about a patchwork family and a pet that couldn't be cuter or sweeter - Mappys.

Mila Albery craftily narrates the fantastic tale from the perspective of the lively ten-year-old Charlie, engaging the young and adult reader to enter the adorable world of Mappys. Her words bring fantasy a step closer to reality, with flowing and easy to read narration that always accentuates the humorous aspects of life.

Mila Albery lives with her family in Vienna, Austria.

Made in United States
Orlando, FL
24 April 2024